To Don (my rock) and Jazzi, Chloe, Zach, Maddy, and Nick—look what Mama did!
And to my Grandma Nell, who could really wear a hat
—M.T.D.

To my wife, Connie, and my daughter, Nia
—F.M.

lara B. was in a hurry. Most Sundays she didn't care where she sat in church, since she spent her time coloring and eating the "be-patient mints" Mama passed her.

Today she cared. It was the third Sunday of the month—Mother's Sunday—when the older ladies dressed in crisp white suits and wore clean white gloves . . . and hats. Big, bold, beautifully colored hats. Then all those hats sat side by side, perched together on the heads of the ladies in the front pews.

Clara B. rushed to claim the seat behind the best hat.

That hat belonged to Grandma. Grandma called it her good hat, and she wore it only on Mother's Sunday. When people complimented Grandma on the hat, she'd just wave her hand and say, "Honey, I'm not wearing this hat. This hat is wearing *me*!"

Every Mother's Sunday Clara B. would ask to wear the hat, but Grandma would always say no. She would offer Clara B. any other hat in her closet, but she'd always say the good hat was "too delicate to be touched by many hands."

Clara B. would sit behind Grandma, and if the hat swayed during the choir's hymn, Clara B. swayed. If the hat nodded forward in agreement with the pastor's message, she nodded, too. And if the hat tipped back so Grandma could laugh at the deacon's comments, Clara B. tipped her head *way* back.

Today she got every movement perfect.

Today that hat is going to wear ME, thought Clara B.

After service, she pushed through the crowd to Grandma's side.
"You want to come and help me shop for Sunday supper?" asked Grandma.

Clara B. nodded. She ran and told Mama, then returned to Grandma's side and
waited. She waited while Grandma chitchatted with the other ladies,

while Grandma shopped at Dominic's Market,

and while Grandma put her coat, purse, and gloves in the hall closet when they finally arrived at her house.

But Grandma didn't take off her hat.

Clara B. grabbed Grandma's hand and pulled her up to the bedroom. Clara B. leaned into the closet and hunted for the pink-and-purple hatbox. "You want me to put the hat away for you?" she asked.

"Sure," Grandma replied, smiling as she started pulling pins from the hat.

Clara B. waited.

Grandma reached for the hat on her head.

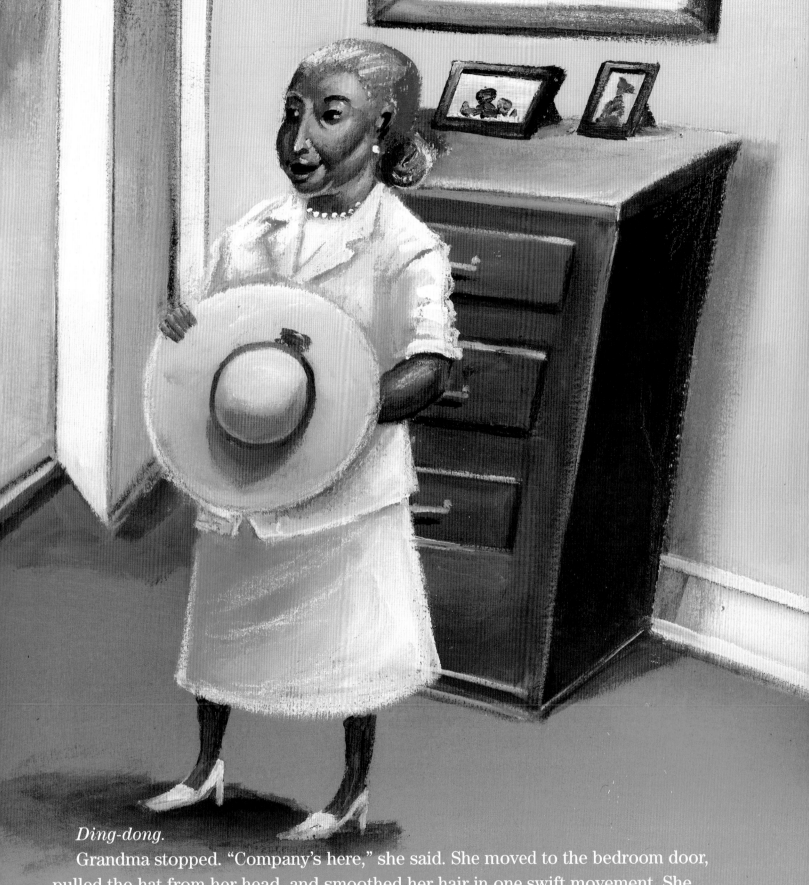

Ding-dong.

Grandma stopped. "Company's here," she said. She moved to the bedroom door, pulled the hat from her head, and smoothed her hair in one swift movement. She carried the hat with her.

Clara B. looked at the box and sighed. She plopped the box on the carpet next to the door and rushed to follow Grandma downstairs . . .

Clara B. trailed Grandma to the kitchen, staring wistfully at the hat as she went.
Grandma tied an apron around her waist and began frying the ham and dressing.
The hat stayed on the table.

At supper, Clara B. didn't really see the food on her plate. She was thinking of ways to get to the hat.

She finally finished eating. She hadn't tasted a thing. She said her "Excuse me's" and started to ease into the family room on tippy toes.

Grandma tapped her shoulder. "Help me with the dishes?" she asked.

Clara B. gasped as she spun to face Grandma. "Yes, ma'am," she replied quickly. She glanced into the family room. The hat still sat on the table. She followed Grandma to the sink with heavy steps.

Drying while Grandma washed, Clara B. peeked at her grandma from the corner of her eye. *Did Grandma know that Clara B. was going to be worn by the hat?* She frowned at the dishes in the sink. She ought to be worn by the hat! She'd done all her Sunday moves perfectly: swaying when the hat swayed, nodding when the hat nodded, tipping way back when the hat tipped back. Finally, all the dishes were clean and Clara B. stepped away from the sink.

Clara B. *deserved* the hat. She walked firmly into the family room. The hat still sat
on the table . . . surrounded by cousins.

Clara B. got mad. *All this waiting, and I'm still not wearing that hat*, she thought.
She began to pace and to plan.

If she had to wait anyway, she might as well watch for the right moment to get that
hat. And Clara B. knew exactly when that would be.

Seven o'clock came. Deacon Thompson said his goodbyes. Mama, Daddy, Auntie, and Uncle gathered around the coffeepot in the kitchen to talk, and the littler cousins spooned together on the sofa and went to sleep.

Grandma walked into the room. "Forgot to put this away," she said, reaching for the hat. "I'll just rest my feet for a second," she added as she eased tiredly into her favorite chair.

Clara B. watched.

Grandma settled the hat in her lap.

Clara B. waited.

Grandma scooted deep into the cushions and gazed out the window.

Clara B. leaned forward.

Grandma yawned, blinked, tilted her head forward, and nodded off to sleep.

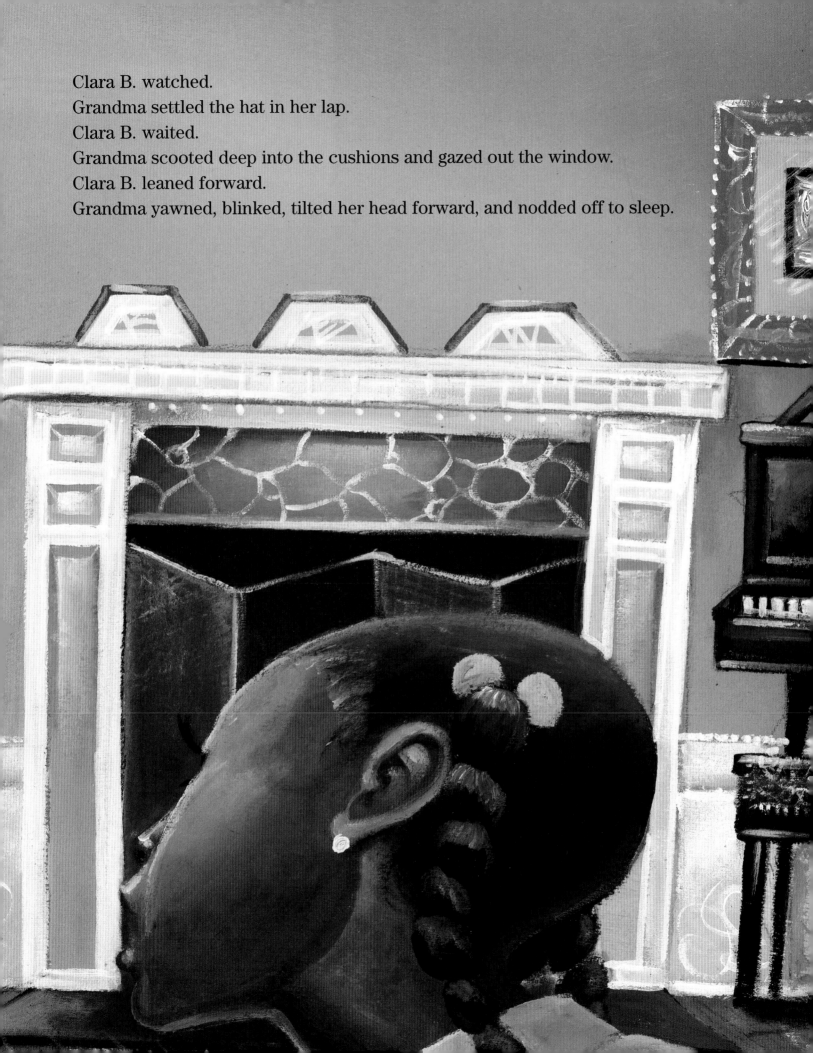

Clara B. carefully approached the chair. She slowly lifted the hat and gently hugged it to her chest. She moved backwards with soft steps, making for the stairs.

Then she ran full force up to the bedroom.

In one excited movement, she pushed open the door, flipped on the light, and stepped into the room.

Her foot landed on the hatbox, tearing the lid.

Before she could get her balance, the box slipped
and carried Clara B. across the carpeted floor. Clara B.
tensed, trying not to scream as she fell.

She landed on Grandma's hat. It was crushed. She
tried to reshape it, but only made it worse.

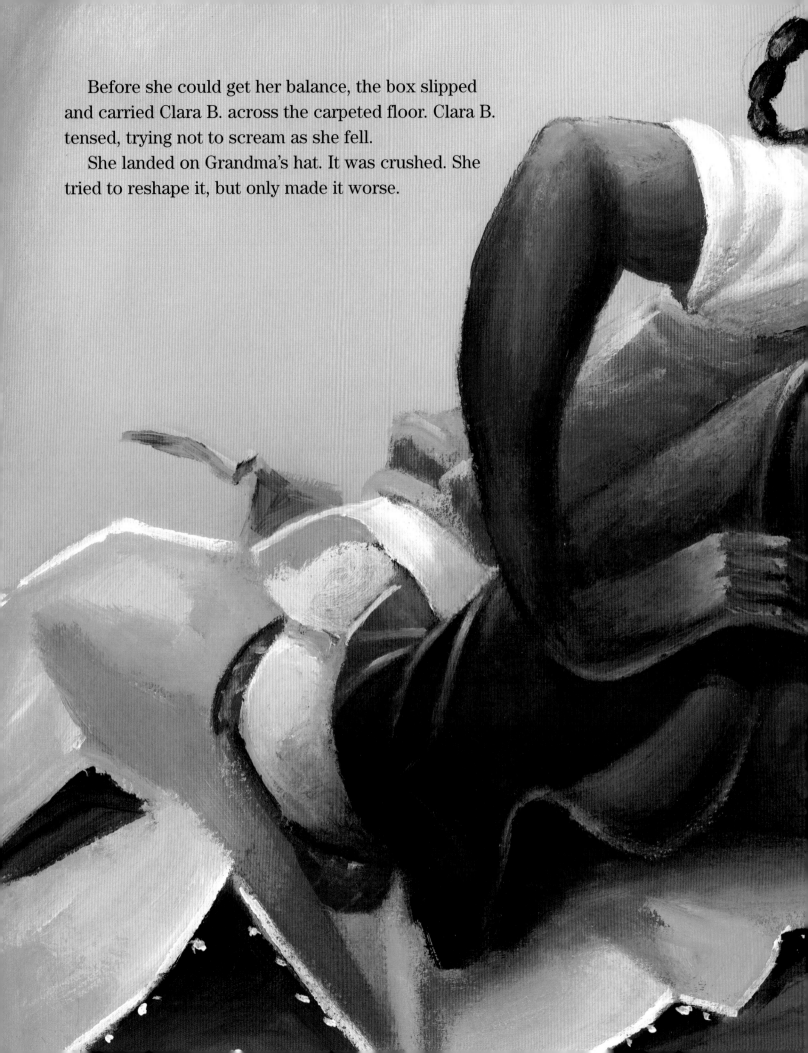

Sitting on Grandma's bed, she buried her sniffles in the quilt. Her fingers played with the cover's knotted string as she wondered how she would tell Grandma.

Clara B. remembered watching Grandma sew a crazy quilt. "My hands do the work, but the quilt tells me when the work's done," Grandma had said.

Clara B. knew how to fix the hat.

She pulled supplies from Grandma's craft drawer. She snipped, glued, cut, and tied, working until the hat told her it was done. She set the new hat in the box and taped the tear in the lid. She paused before putting the lid back on the hatbox.

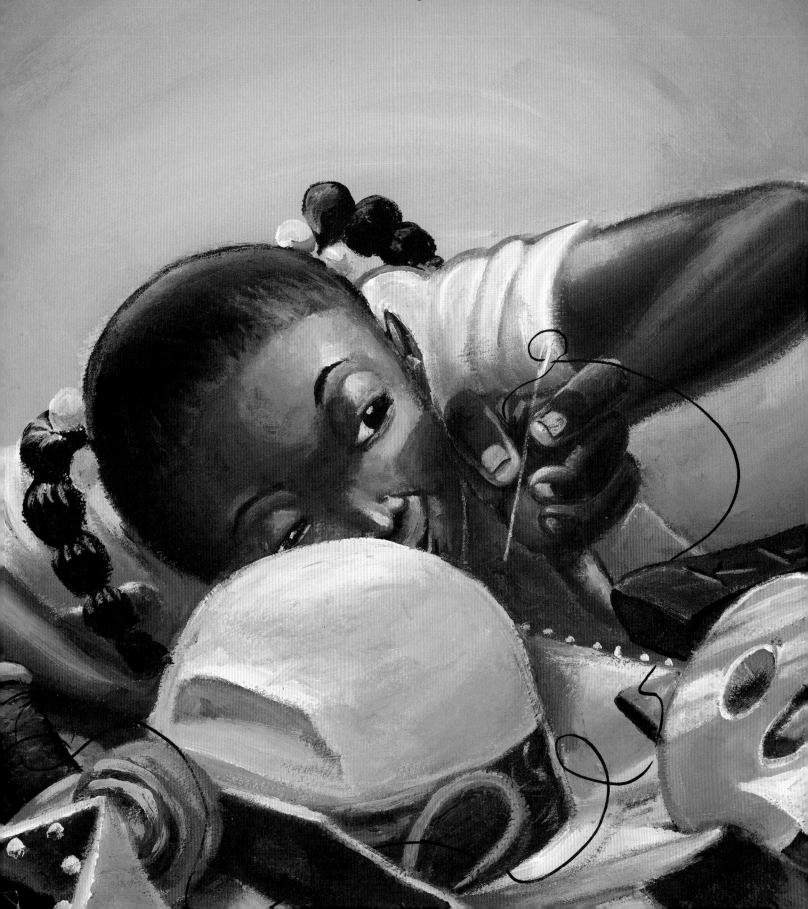

She needed to write Grandma a note. Clara B. got a piece of paper and a pen from Grandma's bedside table. She carefully printed "S-O-R-R-Y" in black ink. Then she put the box back in Grandma's closet.

And she waited once more, but Grandma didn't say anything. Finally, it was Mother's Sunday again.

Clara B. followed her parents into church. She wanted to find Grandma and see if she was wearing the new Mother's Sunday hat, but she was afraid. Instead, she looked down at her dragging feet and let her mother lead the way to the seat.

"Watch where you're sitting," Mama said.
Clara B. looked behind her. A round pink hatbox
marked *Child's Medium* was in her seat. She looked
at Mama.
Mama nodded.

Reaching inside, Clara B. found a hat—bright pink, with soft netted material that gathered into a pink rose. It looked just like Grandma's old good hat.

"Tell Grandma thank you," Mama said.

Clara B. slowly turned and lifted her eyes to the front pew. Grandma was wearing the fixed-up Mother's Sunday hat!

Smiling at Grandma, Clara B. put on her new hat. "Thank you," she said.

"Well now," said Grandma, "you are surely wearing that hat."

"No, ma'am," said Clara B. "This hat is wearing *me*!"

Grandma patted her Mother's Sunday hat and smiled. "Mine too, little 'un," she said. "Mine too."

Author's Note

Mother's Sunday is a tradition that is practiced in many African American Baptist churches. It usually occurs with Communion Sunday—the day the congregation receives Communion. On Mother's Sunday, the older women of the church will dress in their finest white suits and most beautiful Sunday hats. They are escorted to seats of honor in the first few pews of the church. They receive their Communion first and are the first to leave the building when the service is over. Mother's Sunday was practiced before Mother's Day became an official holiday. It is still popular today.